Alexander and the Wind-Up Mouse

ISBN 0-590-43012-2
Copyright © 1969 by Leo Lionni.
All rights reserved. Published by Scholastic Inc., 730 Broadway, New York,
NY 10003, by arrangement with Alfred A. Knopf, Inc.

62 61 60   8 9/0

Printed in the U.S.A.   23

First Scholastic printing, September 1989

Alexander and the Wind-Up Mouse

by Leo Lionni

SCHOLASTIC INC.

New York Toronto London Auckland Sydney

"Help! Help! A mouse!" There was a scream. Then a crash.
Cups, saucers, and spoons were flying in all directions.

Alexander ran for his hole as fast as his little legs would carry him.

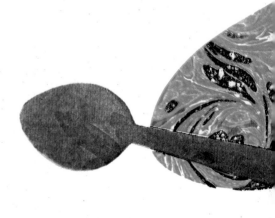

All Alexander wanted was a few crumbs and yet every time they saw him they would scream for help or chase him with a broom.

One day, when there was no one in the house, Alexander heard a squeak in Annie's room. He sneaked in and what did he see? Another mouse.
But not an ordinary mouse like himself. Instead of legs it had two little wheels, and on its back there was a key.

"Who are you?" asked Alexander.

"I am Willy the wind-up mouse, Annie's favorite toy. They wind me to make me run around in circles, they cuddle me, and at night I sleep on a soft white pillow between the doll and a woolly teddy bear. Everyone loves me."

"They don't care much for me," said Alexander sadly. But he was happy to have found a friend. "Let's go to the kitchen and look for crumbs," he said.

"Oh, I can't," said Willy. "I can only move when they wind me. But I don't mind. Everybody loves me."

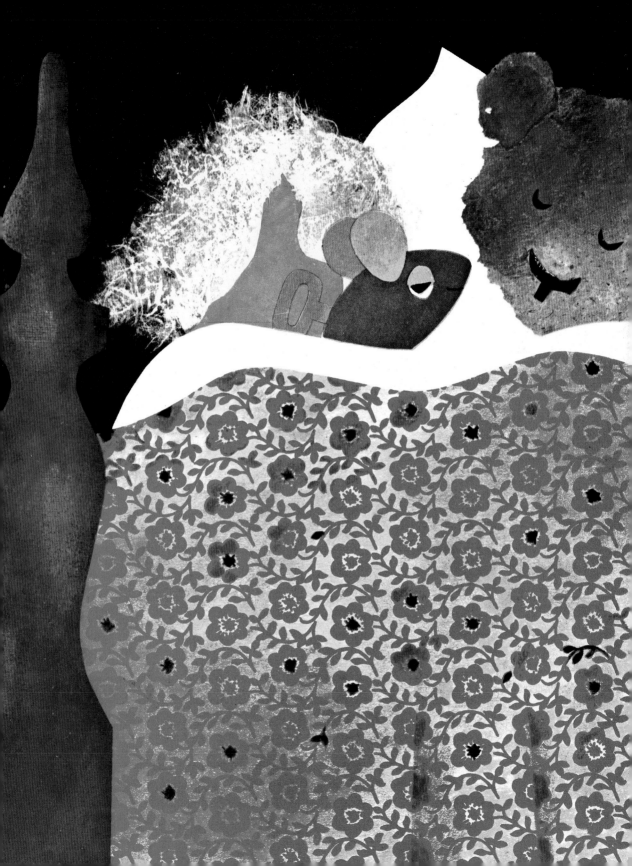

Alexander, too, came to love Willy. He went to visit him whenever he could. He told him of his adventures with brooms, flying saucers, and mousetraps. Willy talked about the penguin, the woolly bear, and mostly about Annie. The two friends spent many happy hours together.

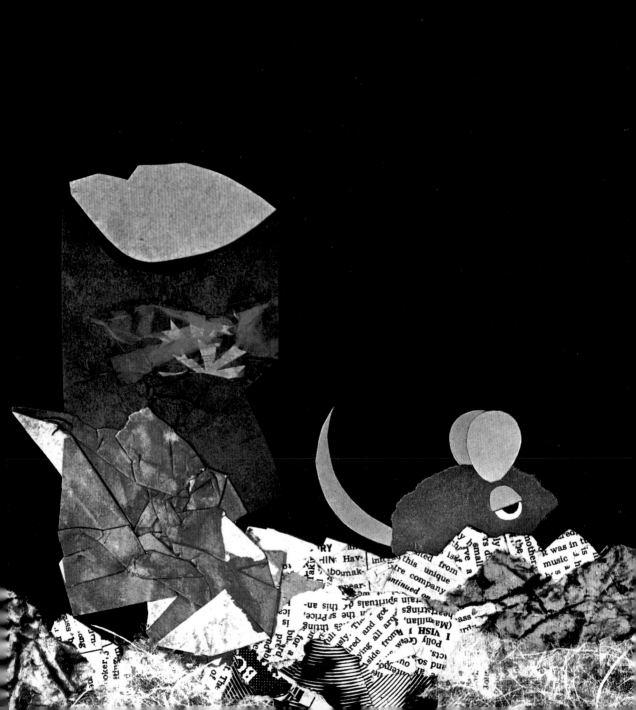

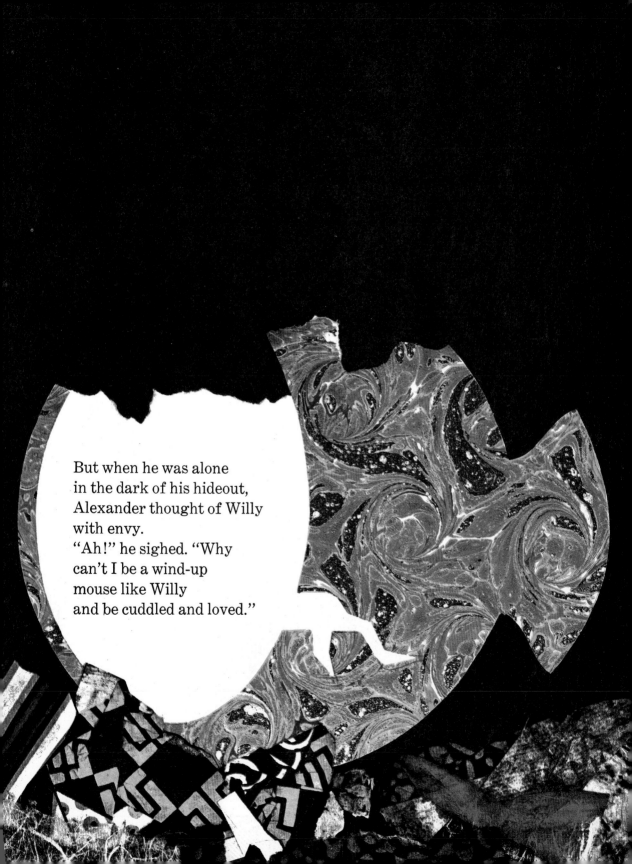

But when he was alone
in the dark of his hideout,
Alexander thought of Willy
with envy.
"Ah!" he sighed. "Why
can't I be a wind-up
mouse like Willy
and be cuddled and loved."

One day Willy told a strange story. "I've heard," he whispered mysteriously, "that in the garden, at the end of the pebblepath, close to the blackberry bush, there lives a magic lizard who can change one animal into another."

"Do you mean," said Alexander, "that he could change me into a wind-up mouse like you?"

That very afternoon Alexander went into the garden and ran to the end of
the path. "Lizard, lizard," he whispered. And suddenly there stood
before him, full of the colors of flowers and butterflies, a large lizard.
"Is it true that you could change me into a wind-up mouse?" asked Alexander
in a quivering voice.

"When the moon is round," said the lizard, "bring me a purple pebble."

For days and days Alexander searched the garden for
a purple pebble. In vain. He found yellow pebbles and
blue pebbles and green pebbles—but not one tiny
purple pebble.

At last, tired and hungry, he returned to the
house. In a corner of the pantry he saw a box full of
old toys, and there, between blocks and broken dolls,
was Willy. "What happened?" said Alexander, surprised.

Willy told him a sad story. It had been Annie's birthday.
There had been a party and everyone had brought a gift.
"The next day," Willy sighed, "many of the old toys were
dumped in this box. We will all be thrown away."

Alexander was almost in tears. "Poor,
poor Willy!" he thought. But then
suddenly something caught his eye.
Could it really be . . . ? Yes it was!
It was a little purple pebble.

All excited, he ran to the garden, the precious
pebble tight in his arms. There was a full moon.
Out of breath, Alexander stopped near the
blackberry bush. "Lizard, lizard, in the bush,"
he called quickly. The leaves rustled and
there stood the lizard. "The moon is round,
the pebble found," said the lizard. "Who or
what do you wish to be?"

"I want to be . . ." Alexander stopped.
Then suddenly he said, "Lizard, lizard,
could you change Willy into a mouse like me?"
The lizard blinked. There was a blinding
light. And then all was quiet. The purple pebble
was gone.

Alexander ran back to the
house as fast as he could.

The box was there, but alas it was empty. "Too late," he thought, and with a heavy heart he went to his hole in the baseboard.

Something squeaked! Cautiously Alexander moved closer to the hole. There was a mouse inside. "Who are you?" said Alexander, a little frightened.

"My name is Willy," said the mouse.

"Willy!" cried Alexander. "The lizard . . . the lizard did it!"
He hugged Willy and then they ran to the garden path.
And there they danced until dawn.